PRAISE ℰ CB SAMET

Four-time award-winning author

"... women engagingly contend with otherwordly entities and real-world danger, while also grappling with that most mysterious phenomena: the human heart. Samet's prose vacillates skillfully between various registers, expressing sensuality, suspense, and humor, as needed.

A collection of well-executed ... tales of love and ghosts."

— KIRKUS REVIEWS (ON ROMANCING THE SPIRIT SERIES, NOVELLAS 1-6)

"[Romancing the Spirit Series: books 1-7] packs an emotional punch, with vivid characters, well-thought-out plots, and unusual paranormal twists."

— JAMIE BEE (BOOKBUB REVIEWER)

Chloe's Cupid

ROMANCING THE SPIRIT SERIES

CB SAMET

Romancing the Spirit

cbsamet.com

© 2020 Avant Star Publishing

Cover Design by: Get Covers

A ROMANCING THE
SPIRIT NOVELLA

CHLŒ'S CUPID

CB SAMET

One

Chimes filled the air with gentle music as Chloe walked into the dimly lit Busy Broomstick. The smell of jasmine incense filled the air. Twinkling golden lights lined the periwinkle walls and dark mahogany shelves. Rows of labeled bottles were stacked together in bright pinks, purples, and blues.

As Chloe's eyes adjusted to the lighting, she read the labels of aromatherapy scented jars on one row—lavender, vanilla, peppermint, passion fruit, and more. The next row had similar fragranced lotions, and the next had matching scented candles.

The opposite wall held spell books with gold lettering and faded spines. A potpourri of ingredients surrounded them—dried fruits, nuts, mushrooms, herbs, and flower petals.

She paused. This was ludicrous. She should turn back around and leave this store. But she was desperate.

"Can I help you?" a woman asked.

Chloe faced the woman behind the counter. "You're Rose? Emma's aunt?"

"Ah, you must be Chloe." Rose wore a long, purple cotton dress, embellished with lace and sequins. The lightweight material was ideal for a California summer. Her dark braided hair contained purple feathers, and her eyes were rimmed in midnight black eyeliner with dark, smoky eyeshadow.

Chloe straightened. "Yes."

Rose walked to the front of the store, locked the door, and flipped the OPEN sign to CLOSED.

"Let's sit down and discuss your dilemma." Rose gestured to a pair of high-back, velvet cushioned chairs.

Chloe sat, tucked a strand of brown hair behind her ear, and clasped her hands in her lap. She fidgeted with the seam of her baby-blue yoga pants.

Rose glided to a table and dispensed hot tea from a large insulated thermos into two small dainty cups with pink flowers and gold fleur de lis. She handed the cup to Chloe.

"Thank you." Chloe sipped. Chamomile. She probably shouldn't drink something that might make her sleepy first thing in the morning, but her nerves appreciated the soothing, warm liquid.

Rose gently sat and crossed one leg over the other. Her relaxed demeanor helped calm Chloe's angst.

"Now, how can I help?"

Since Emma had referred Chloe to the Busy Broomstick, Chloe would see this through. She could back out at any time, she reminded herself.

"My wedding is a week away," Chloe began.

"Congratulations."

"My *third* wedding."

"Oh, my."

"To the same man." Chloe sighed, turning the cup on its saucer in her hand. "See, we've been engaged for two years. We planned to have our first wedding in Hawaii—destination and island paradise all in one—but the Kīlauea volcano erupted. For our second attempt at marriage, we opted for a ski lodge—no danger of volcanoes, or tropical storms. But, unfortunately, I got appendicitis. *Whoosh*—off to the hospital for emergency laparoscopic surgery. At least all the guests had travel insurance for that one."

"You're worried about the third attempt," Rose said, nodding sagely.

"Yes. I mean, I know third time's a charm, but I'm at my wits' end here. We're staying local for the wedding, but Zack travels for work. He flies back tonight, so what could possibly go wrong? Right?" Chloe gave a nervous chuckle before taking another sip of tea. More of an undignified gulp.

"What did you have in mind that I might be able to do?" Rose smiled warmly.

"I don't know." Chloe didn't even know what Rose *could* do. Her friend, Emma, had said only that her aunt dealt with the supernatural and maybe could help. Chloe wouldn't be here if she wasn't so desperate to make the wedding happen.

She continued, "I have no idea what you're capable of doing or how it could possibly help. I'm willing to be put in a hypnotic trance if it would help me to stop worrying. Maybe you have tarot cards that would predict our happily ever after —not that I'm naive enough to equate marriage with happily ever after. I know relationships take nurturing and work. But getting married has been a wicked hurdle we haven't cleared." Chloe pressed her lips together, determined to stop rambling.

Rose gave her another warm and patient smile. "I don't induce trances or predict fortunes, but I think I can help. I'll make you a tincture of belladonna, rose petals, lavender, rosemary, cinnamon, and cloves. After you drink the potion, you'll be able to see a ghost for seven days."

"A ghost?" Chloe asked, sounding skeptical and trying not to sound rude.

"Not just any ghost. Cupid."

She choked on her next sip of tea. "As in arrow through the heart, Cupid?"

"Yes."

"But you said *ghost*, not mythical creature." She set down her cup of tea on a small table beside the chair.

"Yes. Cupid is quite an ancient ghost. His life was filled with love and loss. Now, as a ghost, he helps others find love —perpetuating the stories about him. But there are several points you need to be aware of if you choose to go through with this. First, you will be the only one who can see and hear him. True mediums who can interact with ghosts regularly are rare. My tincture creates a link that normally doesn't exist. Second, Cupid will only help those with pure intentions—you must love Zack, and he must love you. Cupid doesn't trick anyone. No shenanigans."

"No shenanigans." Chloe nodded. She had zero doubts about the fortitude of her and Zack's love. She only wanted to ensure they actually tied the knot this time.

"Third, you need to have the mental fortitude to handle

a ghost in your life for seven days. No mental breakdowns. If you can't handle Cupid's presence, he'll disappear, and so will any help he can provide."

"Help?"

"Yes. And this is important to remember. Cupid can't affect his surroundings—not beyond a few supernatural gusts of wind or flickering lights. But he can see glimpses of the future and guide you to help make your happy day come true."

Chloe felt her skepticism rising along with her heart rate. At least skepticism about ghosts wasn't one of Rose's rules. Chloe locked a congenial smile in place as she contemplated the ludicrousness of taking a potion to see a ghost who'd supposedly help ensure her wedding would take place.

For real this time.

Rose stood, retrieved something from beneath her cash register counter, and returned to Chloe. The strange, elegant woman set a box—ornately decorated in tiny gems and shaped like a miniature treasure chest—on the table beside Chloe's tea cup. After withdrawing a key from around her neck, she unlocked the chest and retrieved a small pink vial from the velvet cushion within the box.

Well, Rose is nothing if not dramatic, Chloe thought.

She accepted the vial. "How much does it cost?"

Rose gave her a pitying look. "For a friend of the family with your bad luck ... nothing. I only ask that if you decide not to use it before your wedding day, please return it to me."

Chloe, now standing, stared down at the vial in her

hand. "K-k. Thank you for this, and for taking the time to meet with me."

"K-k?" Rose asked.

"It's my slang for okay."

"Ah." Rose led her to the door. "If you have any questions, you know where to reach me. Oh, and don't mind his accent. It's a remnant of the Victorian era, though not as flowery."

Because Chloe had no idea how to respond, she gave a weak smile as she left.

If this potion worked, Chloe could tell Zack and they'd both have a good laugh. If it didn't work, she might never admit she'd visited a mystic for help and walked away with a mysterious potion in her hand.

She wasn't sure what terrified her more—that the potion might work... or that it might not.

After Chloe left, Cupid sat down in the chair she'd occupied. He leaned back, crossed his legs, and looked at her partially consumed cup of tea. Rose sipped her own tea and acknowledged his presence with a slight nod of her head.

"Do you think she'll drink it?" Cupid asked.

The young woman who'd scurried out of Rose's shop clearly didn't believe in ghosts.

Rose's eyes twinkled through her heavy make-up. "I'm not sure. She definitely doesn't believe in the paranormal, but then they never do. However, she might be desperate enough to try anything."

Cupid strummed his fingers on his blue jeans. He

hadn't had an assignment in months, and hoped to have one now, but—"You've given me an easy one. A soft pitch, as Americans call it. I call it a doddle.. She's already in love and already has a wedding date. All I have to do is a little handholding for a few days."

"Is that what you see in her future?"

"No. I haven't looked. There's no point in bothering to look unless she actually asks for my help by drinking the potion." And sometimes looking meant seeing only heartbreak.

"Must be hard to know what the future holds, because her repeated efforts to be married have been met with many surprises."

"If she faces some other disasters in proximity to her wedding, maybe she needn't bother to try." He tossed the words out lightly just to antagonize Rose.

"That's an unbecoming thing for the ghost of love to say," Rose scolded lightly. Maybe she's in danger of giving up," Rose countered calmly, "and she needs a little nudge from a ghost."

"We'll see what she decides—play it safe or into the rabbit hole."

A faint breeze curled the pages of a spellbook.

Somewhere across the city, Cupid sensed a choice was already unfolding.

"So, that's where we're at. Five little days away from finally getting married," Zack said.

The gray haired woman in the seat beside him smiled

sweetly. "Quite a story. I do hope it works out for the two of you this time."

When his plane touched down at the San Francisco airport, he felt excitement rise in him. As it taxied, he sent a quick text to Chloe.

Landed. Be home at 8.

"Nothing can go wrong," he told the woman. "We're keeping the wedding local. My fiancée is at home. The plane just landed. The June weather is perfect right now. Everything is set."

Chloe texted back immediately. *K-k.*

He knew she was worried about his travel plans—flying to Dallas and back home so close to the wedding. And rightly so. Their third attempt at a wedding was approaching. They'd made a pact to have no travel plans or strenuous activity the week before the wedding. For him, that meant being cognizant of his work schedule. For her, that meant no vigorous sparring with clients.

Zack enjoyed his job in cybersecurity, but it often meant traveling to the places where his company had been hired. Not everything could be set up remotely when it came to securing data.

Chloe ran her own gym where she taught spin-bike, yoga, and Taekwondo classes. When Zack had met her, she was teaching a self-defense class.

Admittedly, at that first encounter, he hadn't known she was a smart, funny entrepreneur. He'd first noticed her compact body, brunette curls, and dimpled cheeks. She had an adorable smile that crinkled her nose and squinted her eyes.

When he reached Ground Transportation, he withdrew

his phone to connect with a ride share. He'd have an hour in traffic so he hoped he'd be able to get more work done on the trip home.

A prickling sensation crept up his neck—the feeling of being watched.

Nerves, he told himself. Wedding-week nerves.

"Zachary Sumner, come with us. Quietly." Two men flanked him on either side.

"What?"

"We have Chloe, and you need to come with us if you want her to stay safe."

"Chloe?" Zack's heartbeat doubled as he tried to process the threat around him.

Even as they spoke, the large men in black fatigues were already leading him toward a parked green Jeep. Were they police? Military?

"Who are you? I need to see some identification," Zack demanded, blood pumping with fear.

"Get in and don't make a scene." One of the men snatched the phone out of his hand.

They had no identifying logos on their clothing. Their darting eyes looked menacing, and they stunk of sweat and cigarettes.

"Chloe?" Zack's voice constricted even as his mind raced with the hostage training he'd had. The training videos he'd watched did nothing to mimic real danger when everything was moving too fast.

But he couldn't let himself be taken. Catastrophic data breaches could be achieved if someone forced him to share the secrets he knew.

When they reached the vehicle, Zack whirled. "Now

wait a damn minute. I want to see Chloe right *now*." He couldn't fight two kidnappers, but he could make a public scene.

Large arms from inside the vehicle wrapped around him, pulling him into the fold. A noxious smelling rag—presumably chloroform—closed over his mouth, followed by darkness.

Chloe.

He'd never forgive himself if anything happened to her.

Two

After a long day of exercise classes, Chloe arrived home and showered. She left the vial in the kitchen so she could avoid looking at it for a while. She dressed in comfy cotton pants with a matching gray shirt and fluffy pink slippers. An advantage to being a fitness instructor was always wearing comfortable clothes.

The exception was when she needed to pitch a gym membership package to a company for their employees. Getting companies to agree to group rates was part of her specialty. She had the 'pep'—as Zack called it. And once people were inside her facility, she could motivate them. The challenge was keeping them coming back. People led busy lives and struggled to carve out time for wellness— even when they had a group discount and twenty-four hour access.

Blending a kale smoothie, she added protein supplements. She practiced everything she advocated with her clients—low carb, no fake sugar, lots of water and tea.

Chloe's gaze fell on the small pink vial on the kitchen

counter as she drank her health shake. She checked her watch. Zack would be home in thirty minutes. Everything would be fine. She didn't need hocus-pocus potions.

Her phone rang. She jumped, lunged for it, thinking it was Zack, and knocked over her drink. Thick green liquid spread across the counter.

"Dang it!" She answered the phone and put it on speaker as she fetched a towel.

"Hi, Chloe. How are you?"

"Hi, Emma." Not Zack. Chloe tried to conceal the disappointment from her friend.

"My aunt said you visited her this morning."

"No client-mystic privilege, I see," Chloe teased.

"She didn't tell me what she offered you. Did you do whatever it was she advised?"

Chloe mopped up her dinner, picking up the pink vial and cleaning smoothie off of it. "No."

"What? Why not?"

"It's a *potion*. I don't know if it's safe or not. It has belladonna in it."

"So, you might get sleepy. I'm telling you, Rose has helped a lot of people—and not just lovers."

"I don't know. I feel silly about this whole thing."

"Do it. It can't hurt. Oh, my mom's calling in. Gotta go. And please don't leave your maid of honor hanging a third time. Drink for good luck." Emma clicked off.

Guilt rippled through Chloe. Emma had flown to Hawaii and then to the ski lodge without a word of complaint. What was one little drink?

Chloe finished cleaning and drank what was left of her shake, all the while staring at that little pink bottle. The clock on the mantle in the nearby living room ticked by as the weight of silence hung in the room between her and the potion. She drummed her fingers on the counter.

When she checked the time again, she frowned. Zack was fifteen minutes late. She looked at her phone—no calls or text messages. He could be in traffic. Were it not for their track record close to their wedding day, she wouldn't worry at all.

She phoned Zack, but the call went instantly to voice-mail. The pink bottle stared at her. What if something stupid and random ruined them again and she'd done nothing to at least attempt to ward it off? At last, she came to a decision. Worst case scenario was nothing supernatural happened and the belladonna soothed her worry.

She plucked it off the counter, pulled off the cork top, and downed the potion. After downing the surprisingly flavorful drink, she stopped to consider that Rose hadn't given specific instructions—on an empty stomach or with food? In the morning or at night? Maybe it didn't matter.

She waited a moment with bated breath. When nothing happened, she doubled over laughing at herself. "I'm so ridiculous." She wiped at her eyes.

Blinking, her laugh snapped off mid-breath as a translucent figure shimmered into existence before her.

"Hello, Chloe."

Chloe stumbled back, regrouped, and did a round-house kick straight through the figure.

"Good reflexes," he said, voice crisp, clipped, and unmistakably London.

"You're ... you're a ghost!"

"I am the ghost, Cupid, as requested."

The intruder was a young man—perhaps twenty—dressed in jeans and a t-shirt with a cartoon of a plump red heart with an arrow through it. His skin appeared to be a smooth porcelain without a wrinkle or blemish. No wonder he was sometimes depicted as a baby.

"This isn't possible." Her heart raced as she looked around the kitchen for some type of planted projector.

"Your eyes don't deceive you."

Chloe circled Cupid in a careful, defensive pose. Despite teaching Taekwondo, she'd only ever been in one fight where she'd had to defend Emma from a groping drunk at a dance hall.

"You're trespassing," she said.

"You invited me when you drank the potion."

Chloe swiped a hand into the translucent figure, watching it go straight through Cupid.

The ghost yawned. "I can do this all night. In fact, I can do this for eternity. You, however, are on a deadline, if I'm not mistaken."

Chloe stopped circling Cupid as she glanced at the clock. Zack was over an hour late now.

"I want to make sure my wedding happens without any more disasters."

"Hitched without a hitch. Yes, I heard your entire conversation with Rose—she's such a gem. Don't gape at me—just because you couldn't see me up until five minutes ago doesn't mean I don't exist—in the supernatural sense of the word, of course."

Chloe checked her phone again—no call or text from Zack. "So, can you help me?" Her voice had an edge of pleading desperation.

"Because I can see parts of the present others cannot and some of the future, I have been able to unite many couples over the centuries. Usually, it's the little things—flowers, a perfectly timed gift, making impeccable travel plans." His eyes sparkled.

"What do you get out of it?"

"Comfort. Satisfaction and pleasure in knowing I've united lovers. And it passes the time."

"And you're with me for the next seven days?" she asked.

"Seven days or until I'm no longer needed or wanted. I never overstay my welcome."

Chloe paced her kitchen, trying to process how she was having a conversation with a ghost—or perhaps Rose's concoction was a powerful hallucinogenic.

"K-k. I need to test this."

Cupid rolled his eyes.

"Tell me exactly what Emma is doing right now," Chloe said.

Closing his eyes, Cupid pinched the bridge of his nose. "Your friend, Emma, is on her way to the movie theatre with Nick to see the latest superhero blockbuster."

"What!" Chloe snatched up her phone and speed dialed her friend.

Emma answered.

"Are you with Nick?" Chloe demanded.

"How did you know?"

"I thought we decided he was a jerk and you weren't going to give him a second chance."

"I changed my mind," Emma said.

"By taking him to the movie you and I were going to see together?"

"I'm sorry. You've been tied up with wedding plans. Wait. How did you—?"

"Never mind. Enjoy the show, but don't trust Nick."

"Wait, Chloe—"

But Chloe was already disconnecting the call. She set down the phone as she leaned on the counter and closed her eyes to stop the room from spinning. K-k. She could do this. There was no harm in maximizing her chances of wedding success through utilization of this paranormal encounter to its fullest extent.

Her eyes fluttered open, and she scrutinized Cupid's appearance. "No bow and arrow? No wings?"

He crossed his arms. "Nor am I a god as Roman and Greek mythology would have you believe. I used to carry arrows and a torch—symbols of how love wounds and inflames the heart, but I modernized." He gestured at the cartoon heart with an arrow through it on his t-shirt. "I discovered that people of the twenty-first century don't trust young men in togas."

"K-k, Cupid, can you tell me where Zack is?"

"Are you saying you're a believer?"

"I'm saying, I'm less of a skeptic."

"I like honesty. Give me a moment." He closed his eyes again. His face went lax before his brows knitted in together and his lips dropped into a frown. "No, no. This makes no sense."

"What is it? What's wrong?"

"Wait. Give me some context clues right now. Where should your fiancé be?"

"Driving home from the airport. He usually takes a ride share."

Cupid's brow furrowed deeper. "So there's no reason he'd be tied to a chair in a dark room?"

Chloe gasped as she went rigid with fear. "No! What are you seeing?"

"You'll have to excuse me for moment. I need to explore Zack's surroundings to learn more." With that, Cupid vanished, leaving her alone and worried.

The kitchen felt suddenly colder.

Zack was out there somewhere, tied to a chair in the dark.

ZACK WOKE to the obnoxious odor of what he assumed was smelling salts. He recoiled only to feel his arms bound to a chair. He rolled his neck to loosen an ache as his eyes adjusted to a small, dark room with a single ceiling light and heavy curtains over the windows.

He'd been dreaming of Chloe—a vivid re-enactment of when they'd first met.

"Wake up!" a gruff voice commanded.

The awful sulfur smell filled his nostrils again. His eyes focused on a man in a ski mask. Another masked man was a few steps behind him. Were the masks necessary? He'd already seen their faces at the airport.

"Chloe? Where's my fiancée?"

"Alive. For now."

What was the accent? German perhaps. Was he doing business with any German companies? Not recently.

"We need your cooperation, Mr. Sumner, to maintain her safety."

"Cooperation with what?"

"Backdoor access to True Health's medical records. You were the cybersecurity specialist on their team. You helped build their system."

"Why do you want access? Those are people's health records." But Zack knew the answer.

He'd heard the rumors in the tech world that a health conglomerate's database had been hacked. Those infil-trating had held the access to information for ransom—threatening to leak personal health information electroni-cally. *Globally*. Rather than face public disgrace, loss of clients and investors, and ultimate bankruptcy, the company had paid the ransom money to have the data breach sealed by the very perpetrators who'd opened it.

This felt exactly like that—and he was the tool they wanted.

"Your cooperation, Mr. Sumner."

"Let me speak to Chloe. I want to know she's safe." He'd promised no travel this close to the wedding. One last quick trip, he'd argued. One last quick payday. God, what a mistake.

The man reared back and punched Zack in the jaw. Pain exploded through his face as the taste of blood filled his mouth. Lights and stars swam before his eyes.

"Hey!" the other man snapped. "Not the face. And not the hands. We can't risk damaging his sight or his ability to type." This other masked man was dressed in slacks, a button-down shirt, and loafers. He smelled of expensive cologne.

Zack couldn't place the men. He certainly had never met them before.

"Then, why didn't we grab the woman from the start? This guy isn't going to cooperate without coercion," the brute complained.

Through the pain, Zack concentrated on their words. So they didn't have Chloe. Had they lied to get Zack to comply?

"We planned to pick up Mr. Sumner's fiancée at their home while we picked up Mr. Sumner from the airport. Unfortunately, those men were stuck in traffic. But they should have her any moment. She'll be here soon. In the meantime, I'll try to appeal to Mr. Sumner's financial tastes."

Loafers turned toward Zack. :If you can't be bribed, then we'll see how much you value your betrothed."

Zack's stomach sickened. He would cave if they produced Chloe, he knew he would. Whatever they wanted —code written for access to the health records, build a platform to export data, build a website to post the information for their ransom scheme. Any of it in exchange for Chloe unharmed.

But they didn't have her in custody yet, and that gave him a glimmer of hope. She was a petite five-five—all slender muscles from endless days of teaching exercise classes. She also knew Taekwondo. These men had her beat by size but maybe not skill. And certainly not spunk.

Except, she'd be home alone right now. And the kidnappers probably had weapons.

There was another enormous problem—Chloe loved Zack. If the two men picking her up told her to come or harm would befall her fiancé, she'd accompany them without hesitation.

Zack figured he had maybe a few hours to devise a way for both of them to escape, because if they didn't, these men were unlikely to leave them alive after they got what they wanted.

Three

Chloe paced her kitchen, waiting for Cupid to return. Waiting for a ghost. She shook her head in disbelief.

Seven days.

She only needed him for five. Just to make sure the wedding happened. She wasn't crazy. She was desperate. Desperate times, desperate measures and all that.

Cupid reappeared, looking distraught.

"What's wrong?" Her heart thudded with worry.

"Zack has been kidnapped."

"Kidnapped? I don't understand. Why would he be kidnapped?"

Cupid pinched the bridge of his nose. "I saw... a group of international thieves. They want his cybersecurity skills to break into True Health's data. Ransom, blackmail—the whole rotten lot."

Chloe clasped her hands to her mouth. Zack had said something like this was a possibility in his line of work. There were protocols. She was supposed to go to the police.

Her knees went weak. For one dizzy heartbeat she couldn't move at all. Then training and terror kicked in together.

She raced upstairs and began packing. According to the company's safety protocol, she had to leave the house and not return until it was safe. She needed at least an overnight bag.

Cupid watched her frantic motions. "I was going to tell you to pack and leave, but it seems you're already aware."

"Aware? Aware of what?" Her voice was breathless from fear and exertion.

"The thieves intend to kidnap you next to use you as leverage to make Zack comply."

Chloe stuffed jeans and shirts into a bag. "Is he hurt? No, don't tell me. He's alive. That's all that matters." She dumped toiletries in the bag. Still in the bathroom, she put on her work clothes she'd set aside for the following day. Pausing and without making eye contact, she asked again, "Is he hurt?"

"Just scratches and bruises."

Chloe sniffed as she zipped her bag shut. She lugged it to the kitchen where she filled a plastic bottle with tap water. "I have to go to the police."

Cupid scratched his head, not ruffling his perfectly waved crop of hair. "This is all a bit beyond my purview."

"I can't go to the police." Eyes wide with realization, she turned to look at the ghost—through the ghost. "I have no proof he's been kidnapped. I can't tell them a ghost told me, and even though the twenty-four hours missing rule is actually a myth, Zack is only late by over an hour. No one will believe me. And I can't risk his safety by waiting."

Cupid shuffled his feet. "I'm not really qualified to help with this sort of thing."

Chloe snatched her keys, phone, and charger before heading to her car, her mind racing.

Zack has been kidnapped.

She loaded her bag in the backseat of her Prius and turned to Cupid. "Are you coming?"

"I think Rose should find you the ghost of a former police detective or FBI agent or something. I'm the ghost of love and desire—not rudding kidnapping."

"Oh, no you don't. You're not backing out on me. I've got you for seven days. I don't have time to find another ghost. You agreed to help make my wedding happen, and this is part of it. Hop in ... or whatever it is ghosts do."

Chloe climbed in the driver's seat, closed the door, and buckled in.

"Ghost of love, not Liam Neeson," he grumbled, but he still flickered into the passenger seat. "Are you always this commanding, then?"

"Instructing," she corrected him. "I'm a teacher, so I'm good at instructing."

She pulled out of the driveway. "Where to?" She was a teacher, but also a doer. She didn't run her own gym by shrinking from her fears. Face them. That's what she taught in her classes ... although she would never advise her students to take on a group of kidnappers.

"What do you mean?"

"Where is Zack being held?"

"You're going after him?" Cupid gaped at her.

"Yes."

"In your pink yoga clothes?"

"Yes."

He crossed his arms. "You and what army?"

"Why do you say that? How many are there?"

"Four. And one of you."

"But I have you."

"Take a left here." He waved his hand. "But what if they have guns?"

"We'll need a way to sneak in and sneak out," she replied. She wasn't being reckless, she assured herself. If the situation looked too dangerous, she could at least get proof of his kidnapping and share that with police.

"A spy ghost. What if we find you a former spy?"

"Buck up, Cupid. We're on the clock. Give me the layout of where Zack's being kept."

CHLOE TAPPED her steering wheel while they sat in traffic on Highway 92—on the bridge outside Palo Alto. Nervous energy and worry over Zack rippled through her.

"How'd you become a ghost?" she asked.

"Betrayed love. A broken heart. Proper tragic, really," he said. "There's a medical term for it in modern times— Takotsubo cardiomyopathy—when an emotionally traumatic event causes heart failure. It's not usually fatal these days. It's also uncommon in men, but then I am a hopeless romantic."

"I'm sorry about your heart."

"Ah. That was so long ago. And look at me now—I'm famous, and I help people find love. No piercing arrows involved in the literal sense."

"And you seek nothing in return?" she asked. The conversation helped distract her from her worry over Zack.

Cupid shrugged. "I'm a ghost. I can't do anything with material items. I suppose if I were mean spirited, I could make people leap through hurdles before I helped them, but that's not what love is about."

"How can you help find love? Is it so predictable?"

"I can glimpse the future—see if two people fall in love. But—disclaimer alert—it's up to them to maintain it."

"Have you ever had a request like mine?"

"A kidnapping? No."

Chloe chuckled. "No, I meant two people who love each other but can't seem to tie the knot."

"Twice. One was a man who needed help with the right proposal because his attempts were thwarted by fate. Another was a runaway bride. And there was no chasing her. I can't always give a happily-ever-after..." His voice trailed at the last sentence.

Chloe suspected Cupid was partially referring to a less-than-optimistic outlook on her situation with Zack. She'd fix that. She'd show him how they were meant to be together and the kidnappers were not insurmountable obstacles.

"Zack and I met at a self-defense course."

"Oh? What motivated you to take such a class?"

"I was the instructor."

"Fascinating."

"Yeah, so, we're in my gym, and everyone is dressed in workout clothes, ready to get physical. I try to weave the lecture portions in with hands-on demonstrations. After all, everyone's tired after a long day of work. There are a dozen things they'd rather be doing, so part of my job is to keep the class interesting. Anyway, I notice a man. The *only* man."

"Zack?"

"This guy has a pretty good build, right? Defined arms, flat abs. Tall, dark, handsome. All that and a bowl of whipped cream."

"A bowl of—"

"So, I'm thinking to myself—he's built like that and not wearing a ring while taking a class statistically known to be predominantly filled with women. There's only one reason he's here."

"There is?"

"To pick up women," Chloe explained.

"Ah."

She could envision the event like it happened yesterday as she told Cupid the story. Each person stood on their respective mats—attentive and limber.

She'd already covered a few basic lessons—know your surroundings, don't be distracted, and protect your space.

"Gentleman in the back?" she asked.

He waved.

"Can you volunteer for us?"

He joined Chloe at the front of the room with a surprisingly tentative smile when she'd expected him to eat up the attention.

"Your name?"

"Zack Sumner."

Chloe addressed the group. "Zack is going to be our stand-in demo." She leaned toward Zack. "You signed the waiver at the beginning, right?"

The class laughed.

"I'm just kidding," she chuckled. She leaned closer, dropping her voice to a whisper. "Only half-kidding."

His cheeks flushed.

"Your key attack areas," she announced, circling Zack, "are the eyes, throat, and groin."

Zack's Adam's apple bobbed in an adorable swallow.

"Let's demonstrate that." She took a stance with her back to Zack and one side facing the students. "You grab me from behind, and let's say in this situation we're in a parking garage, so you don't want me to scream. Your hand goes over my mouth."

He wrapped one hand around her in a mock attack where he was two inches from actually touching her. His hand hovered in front of her mouth.

Good-looking, shy, and a gentleman. Maybe she shouldn't have picked on him.

"I can't give you one formula to say—if you're grabbed from behind, do this. The reason is that where you're grabbed and where your attacker's center of balance is will determine your reaction. So we need to go through each scenario. In this one, his hand is over your mouth, like Zack's demonstrating, which means he's going to be pulling you back against him. Don't fight it. You're not stronger than him, so you'll waste energy and probably get hurt in the process. You can't reach his neck or groin if he's pressed against you, but you can reach his—?"

"Eyes," several people said.

"Yes. So, as he pulls your weight back," Chloe leaned back even though Zack seemed too terrified to move and play the part of attacker, "you can shoot your fist—thumb

27

pointed towards his eye—towards your attacker's face. You might not hit the eye, and that's okay. Zack, when you see my fist and thumb coming toward your face, what do you want to do?"

"Back away, duck, or spin away."

"Exactly. Show me."

As she bent her arm at the elbow and brought her thumb jerking toward his eye, he took a step back and twisted slightly.

"Good. Pause right there. Now, class, maybe you hit him in the face or eye and now he's standing like this or maybe he dodged and now you have an opening to his—?"

"Groin."

"Yes. Now it can be a chop with the same arm or a grab, squeeze, and pull down."

She took him through several other demonstrations without ever touching each other as Zack dutifully played the role of the attacker while simultaneously not comfortable with the idea of attacking. She'd expected him to work the crowd a little bit, but he was surprisingly reserved. Had she misjudged his intentions?

When they finished, she asked everyone to give him a round of applause before dismissing the class.

As students packed their belongings and filed out, she approached Zack. "What brings you to a self-defense class?"

"I was mugged. I'm not so upset about the money, but it felt like such a violation of my humanity. I didn't like feeling helpless."

"You don't look helpless." She caught herself looking, really looking for the first time at his trim physique. She started to wish he had touched her during the demonstration but quickly dismissed the thought as unprofessional.

"Having a good weight and cardiovascular routine doesn't mean I know how to defend myself."

"True. And it takes courage to both realize that and come to a class like this."

He grinned. "I didn't know I'd be the only guy."

"I hope you'll come back. I promise not to put you on the spot like that again."

"I don't mind being part of a demonstration. I just didn't want to be the violent offender."

"K-k. Next time, we'll reverse roles and see how much you remember from tonight's lessons."

An impatient horn blared behind them. Chloe checked her mirrors, heart lurching, half-expecting a green Jeep with masked men. Nothing—just a BMW riding her bumper. She exhaled and adjusted her grip on the wheel.

"Was it love at first sight?" Cupid asked.

"Um. No. Is that really a thing? I can see it with shoes. But people?"

"It can be. It doesn't replace the work needed to remain together."

"Duh." Chloe went to nudge Cupid's arm with her elbow, but it went right through him. She threw her head back and laughed—part humor at her bizarre situation and part nerves at driving into the unknown.

Four

Zack sat alone in the dark room, thinking about his future wife. He recalled the unconventional start to his and Chloe's relationship. It had been perfect. Just perfect. It fit Chloe and her unconventional personality.

He'd started taking self-defense classes not only because he'd been mugged—a frightening and infuriating moment where he'd frozen and given the mugger what he'd wanted without even considering putting up a fight—but also because Zack had heard rumors in the cybersecurity world about thieves not having their own hackers and so kidnapping people to do their bidding. Someone with Zack's computer skills could be an asset to someone with dubious intentions.

When he'd returned the second night to self-defense class, Chloe had showed students how to free themselves from several different holds with the attacker standing behind them. But she didn't once call on him to be the victim as she'd said she would do. Instead, she rotated through different women in the group. He'd learned a lot, but he was a little disappointed she hadn't used him for one of her demos again.

He lingered after the lesson to ask Chloe about the change of plans, waiting in the line of women who talked with her. He watched this social butterfly answer questions from defense, to offensive fighting, to health and nutrition. Her light and bubbly personality was in contrast to the depth of knowledge she possessed about overall personal wellness.

By the time he reached the front of the line, he'd forgotten what he'd originally planned to discuss.

"So, magnesium for leg cramps?" he asked, having overheard the last several conversations.

"Yeah. You can get it through leafy vegetables, fruits, and nuts. Or my favorite—dark chocolate. But sometimes you can take a supplement."

He made a mental note to pick up magnesium next time he was grocery shopping. He seemed to cramp on heavier workout days and a banana wasn't cutting it. "Cool. How'd you get into fitness?"

"I could claim it was my really cool older sister who's a doctor, but it probably was the crush I had on my high school gym teacher."

Zack chuckled.

He'd later learned that Chloe not only owned the gym he was standing in, but three others around town. Wellness instructor, Taekwondo first-degree black belt, and entrepreneur.

She bit her lip. "Look, I know I said we'd swap roles in

the demo today, and then I benched you, but I felt bad putting you on the spot last time."

"I didn't mind." He picked up his gym bag and slung it over his shoulder. "I'll be here next time, if you need a victim."

She tilted her head to one side and grinned. Zack left before his flirtatious tone could sink in and the moment turn awkward. He didn't look back as he left. He didn't want to know if her grin had widened or slipped into a frown. He'd find out next week, and by that time, he'd work up the courage to ask her out.

A pipe groaned somewhere in the old house, snapping Zack back to the present. His wrists throbbed against the restraints. He forced himself to breathe evenly.

And yet... remembering Chloe steadied him.

"ARE you always this energetic or only when your fiancé is in trouble?" Cupid asked.

"Always," Chloe answered without hesitation as she tapped her fingers on the steering wheel. "I learned the word *exhausting* at a young age because my parents used it to describe me to other parents. 'We love little Chloe, but she's *exhausting*.' And they'd draw it out as if it had six syllables. Don't get me wrong—they love me. But I was a late in life surprise baby, so my energy level combined with older parents was hard on them. Of course, now that I'm thirty three, independent, and running my own business, they can sit back and enjoy. I'm referred to as *jubilant* rather than *exhausting*."

Cupid chuckled. "And what about Zack? Does he enjoy this energy?"

"I assume so. After all, he still wants to marry me. He's three years younger than me so maybe that's why he doesn't find me *exhausting*."

"Indeed? He's three years younger than you?"

"Yeah, we didn't know that until after our first date, but I already liked him by then. Besides, women live longer than men—maybe we all ought to be picking younger men." She glanced in the rear view mirror for tails.

"Brilliant. Sounds like you've got it all figured out."

She narrowed her eyes at him. "Are you mocking me?"

He raised his hands as if in self-defense. "Not at all. I'm enjoying your *jubilance*. It's very refreshing. This entire experience is quite different from the longing-to-love-whilst-languishing individuals who call on me and imagine that love will fix all of their problems."

"Well, this time, we're fixing love rather than it fixing us."

"Bending it to your will," Cupid mused.

"You bet your heart-tipped arrow. Zack and I tried playing love's game—peaceful wedding planning and anticipating our union. Now, I'm taking the bull by the horns."

"If anyone has the needed tenacity, I believe you, Chloe, are that person." His tone was light, but she sensed the worry beneath it.

As she took I-580W, she passed a billboard for the latest action movie with the hero looking buff and ready to fight. She recalled another class Zack had attended. She'd dressed one of her personal fitness instructors in a padded suit and had the students form a line. One by one, they'd moved through the line, made a punch or kick into the padding, and walked to the back of the line to do it again.

"We're all taught at a young age—no hitting, no biting, no scratching, no throwing things. When you're in a situation with someone who means you harm, those rules go out the window. You do what you need to do to get free and get safe. This exercise is to get you less uncomfortable striking someone so that if a crucial moment to your survival arises, you don't hesitate because you're a decent person programmed since childhood to play nice in the sandbox. Defending yourself doesn't make you a bully or a violent person."

Chloe broke into the line. A redhead stood at the front —Barbara, Chloe recalled her name.

"Now, you're going to kick Rick between the legs."

"What?"

"I assure you, he's well padded. We've been doing this routine for five years."

"Um, okay." Barbara took a ready stance but didn't kick.

Chloe addressed the class. "The good person in you would never do that to a man. The woman—or man— defending herself—or himself—might have to." Chloe turned back to Barbara. "Go ahead."

Barbara kicked. Rick didn't flinch. Some of the other women gasped and others chuckled, but the momentum picked back up and all of the women took their turn— some shy and some with a bit of telling aggression.

Zack stood at the front of the line. "Maybe I'll skip my turn."

"Because you're a guy?" Chloe asked.

"Yeah. It doesn't seem right." He eyed Rick warily.

"Ever seen *Butch Cassidy and the Sundance Kid*? Guys kick other guys when they need to. Remember, your actions are for self-defense."

"Since we're talking movies, you know *Casino Royale*—the James Bond movie? I'm picturing that awful torture scene. I was physically ill watching that."

"Look at Rick. He's fine, ten kicks later."

"And he looks like a decent guy. Probably wouldn't hurt a stray dog."

"K-k." She took a step back from Zack. The purpose of the exercise was to push people out of their comfort zone, but Chloe wouldn't push too far. "Next up?"

The lesson continued. At the end, Chloe had everyone relax on their mats and deep breathe.

When the class was dismissed, Zack approached. "Great class."

"Thanks. I feel like I put you on the spot again."

"We're good." He smiled. "Would you be interested in grabbing a bite to eat?"

"K-k. I'm going with a group of friends to Fuki Sushi. Do you want to join us?"

Noticing the part-startled, part-disappointed expression on his face, Chloe realized Zack had been referring to a date. "Oh, you meant just you and me."

"Well, a group is fine, too. In fact, with you being a black belt, maybe a group would be safer for me to start with."

She chuckled since he was making reference to one of the safety-first rules she'd covered in class—getting to know someone before dating them alone.

Zack had joined her that night with her friends and proved himself very amicable. Three days later, they went on a real date.

"You know, this isn't quite what I do in guiding a love life," Cupid muttered, bring her attention back to the present. "Most people just need help picking a proposal spot."

She tightened her white-knuckled grip on the wheel. "I'm not most people."

～

ZACK TWISTED his wrist against his restraints. How much time had passed? It was hard to gauge, but he hadn't made much progress in his escape plan. His kidnappers still hadn't produced Chloe. He took that as a good sign.

He thought of the first date he and Chloe had gone on. She didn't want a long, drawn out meal, so he'd opted to take her to Red Java's House. After dinner, they'd strolled along The Embarcadero strip of piers.

"Tell me more about cybersecurity. What do you do exactly?" she asked.

He took a chance and reached for her hand. They walked side by side as he felt the warmth from her slender fingers. Her body language remained relaxed, and he wondered if she felt the same zinging chemistry at their touch as he did.

"Cybersecurity is all about protecting online data from being compromised. I safeguard files and networks, and install firewalls. Then, I show medical centers how to create security plans and monitor for internal and external threats."

"Very cool. Sounds pretty intense," she said.

"Not really. It's a lot of code. Long hours at a desk."

"Oh, you could get one of those hinged desks so you can alternate sitting and standing."

"I might look into that." he said.

"And I could show you some stretches you can do at work during your breaks."

The idea of Chloe stretching had Zack forgetting the discomfort of lower back pain. "You own gyms. You're funny and energetic. I have to ask ... you are actually single, right?"

She laughed. "Yes, I'm single. Let's see ... Bobby said I was too high energy. Justin got mad at my suggestions for healthier eating. I mean, the guy was a walking junk food munching machine. He may have been built like Chris Hemsworth, but it's going to eventually catch up to him. And, most recently, Antonio didn't want a woman who could beat him in a fight."

"Was he planning on fighting you?"

"No, but when he learned I was a black belt, he excused himself from the relationship. Oh, this is way more information than I should be sharing on a first date. Which reminds me, Jim said I shared too much."

She started to tug her hand back, but Zack didn't let go. "I like it. I deal with data. You're giving me a data download. Besides, cybersecurity is all about protecting secrets, so I like being with someone who isn't secretive. Also, I like health and high energy. As for beating me in a fight, I'd spar with you anytime and enjoy watching you land me on my backside over and over and over."

She laughed, tucking a strand of dark brown hair behind her ear. He saw a faint blush of her cheeks by the light of the lanterns lining the dock. She looked up at him, blue eyes vibrant from her rosy cheeks.

"Where can I take you on date number two?"

Chloe stopped and leaned on the railing.

Zack followed her gaze out over the ocean. The salty breeze blew through his hair as gulls flew low, looking for their next snack.

"The Zone."

"The laser tag place?" he asked.

"My niece's birthday party is there on Saturday, and the rest of my calendar is full until the following week. And I don't want to wait that long to see you again."

"Laser tag it is."

Chloe bit her lip. "It'll be a rambunctious bunch of twelve-year-olds cracked out on pizza and soda."

"It'll be fun."

Zack had had so much fun, especially watching Chloe fully embrace the role of warrior aunt. With her grace and agility, no one got a shot on her while Zack spent most of his time with his lights alarming that he'd been hit.

A door slammed somewhere in the house and Zack flinched.

What he wouldn't give to be playing tag with Chloe right now instead of tied to a chair, fearing for their lives

Five

"Are you okay?" Cupid looked at Chloe who'd fallen uncharacteristically silent. The night was taking unexpected turns for him, but the ordeal was much harder for her.

"The only fight I've ever been in was over before it started. Emma and I were at a dance club. She was dancing her heart out, and I was drowning in sorrow over missing Hawaii. Zack was out of town on business. Anyway, so this chunky guy with some 1990s boy-band hair waving in the breeze gets all gropey."

"Gropey?" Cupid asked.

"Yes. It's totally a word, and if it isn't, it should be. So, I'm already in a bad mood with two drinks on board."

"Honestly, I'm incapable of picturing you in a bad mood," he mused.

She was so relentlessly chipper. But she also had a protective streak, evidenced by her rush to rescue Zack and now this story which sounded like she was going to rescue Emma.

Chloe gave her most severe scowl, but Cupid only laughed.

"Do go on," he said.

"I stormed onto the dance floor and got in his face. 'My friend obviously doesn't like your frisky fingers, buddy, so get it under control.' Gropey tells me to mind my own business while Emma gets sheepish. 'It's okay, Chloe, let's just go.' But I'm not about to let the situation diffuse, because *it's not okay*. 'Say you're sorry,' I tell Gropey. He smirks and replies back with 'You're just jealous.'"

Cupid listened with captured interest to Chloe's retelling of the events and the way she changed her tone from Gropey's lazy, deep slur to Emma's high-pitched damsel-in-distress.

"'Lay a hand on me, and you'll find out just how *not* jealous I am.' He moves to push me away with one hand because—let's be honest—I was crowding him and picking a fight. I intercept his hand, twist his wrist, and bring him to knees. Emma gasps, and by this time, the dancers are turning into gawkers. 'Say you're sorry,' I tell him again. 'I'm sorry. I'm sorry,' he says, though that's the PG version of what he actually said. As we left, he called me crazy."

A horn blared behind her when she drifted a little in her lane. Chloe corrected, heart pounding, then finished, "As you can see, the entire event unfolded in a completely rational way."

"Completely rational," Cupid replied dryly in that British way that meant the opposite.

When Chloe fell silent again, Cupid stared out the car window at the dark summer sky speckled with stars. What had Rose gotten him into? Of course she had no idea Chloe's situation would become so dangerous.

He was way out of his depth here. He felt the weight of everything in the couple's life riding on his ghostly skills. Normally, if he didn't succeed, two people didn't end up together. Such an outcome could be blamed on the intricacies of finicky love. In Chloe's and Zack's case, a failure on Cupid's part could result in one or both of them harmed or worse.

Chloe's spunk, honesty, energy, and obvious love for Zack had instantly endeared her to Cupid. The ancient ghost desperately wanted to give her the outcome she desired and seemed to deserve.

Much of Cupid's worry came from their heavy reliance on his ability to see the future. The future held thousands of possibilities, each dependent on a chain reaction. They could misstep anywhere along the way and alter the outcome they had hoped and planned for.

Cupid silently vowed to do his best—for both Chloe and Zack.

Failure didn't just mean a broken heart this time—it meant broken bodies.

ZACK TRIED to gauge how much time had passed when his captors came back into his room. Two hours perhaps. He hadn't succeeded in loosening his bonds. Mostly, he was sore and bleeding now.

"Is your fiancée sleeping around?" Brute asked.

"No."

"She's not at your home. Where else would she be at night? A friend's house?"

"You think I'm going to make this easier for you?" Zack laced his voice with venom, even as he felt rising hope that they wouldn't snare Chloe.

She could be any number of places—Emma's house, the movies, her parents' house. She was also probably frantic with worry with the wedding so close and then him not home on time. By now with no communication from him, she would've checked her app to try to track him on his phone, and—assuming his kidnappers had turned it off—she might even already be asking the police to help her. This close to the wedding and the fact that he always called or texted if he was going to be late, would spur her into action.

But would the police do anything other than ask her the same question the kidnappers had asked him: could your fiancée be sleeping around. Of course not, but they might not take her concerns seriously.

Or... she could have already made that assumption and be out looking for him. But she'd never find him. That was a good thing—he didn't want her anywhere near these monsters.

Loafers pulled out his phone and began typing with his thumbs. "Actually, you *are* going to help us. If she isn't cheating on you, then she'll respond to a little SOS text message."

"What?"

"We obtained both of your mobile numbers weeks ago. Cloning phones is far easier than hacking a multilayered security system."

"No!" Zack yelled, squirming in his chair. If they had

cloned his phone, then the text message Loafer's was writing to Chloe would appear to come from Zack's phone.

The man left the room, chuckling and typing. Brute snickered as he followed behind his partner in crime.

Zack tilted his head back, cursing. He had to escape. His ropes hadn't loosened enough to free his hands. When they were free, he had only one exit from the room and no idea the layout of the house. There were at least two kidnappers—both larger than him—and his only weapon was the chair he sat on. He hadn't seen any guns yet, but that didn't mean they weren't armed.

Five days until their wedding. Five days. All he wanted to do was live a blissful life with his effervescent wife, Chloe. Were they destined not to achieve a union?

He recalled their last failed attempt. They'd been packed and ready to fly to the mountains. That night Chloe had complained about an upset stomach. The next morning, she looked pale.

"Honey, maybe we should get you checked out," Zack suggested.

"I'm okay." She loaded her carry-on into the car. "Probably something I ate. It'll pass."

He didn't want to argue with her, so he hefted their suitcases into the trunk, watching her try to hide the abdominal pain she obviously felt.

On the way to the airport, Chloe gasped and grimaced. "This might be bad."

Zack never slowed as he changed routes from the airport to the nearest hospital. The ER did CT scans and told them she had appendicitis before she was whisked away to surgery.

Zack remembered wiping tears from her eyes as she lay on the gurney. "I'll be right here when you wake up."

While she was in surgery, Zack had called her family and cancelled the wedding.

She went from laproscopic surgery in the OR to the recovery room to a hospital room bed. The surgeon told Zack that if she'd been on a plane with a ruptured appendix, Chloe would have had to have emergent open abdominal surgery. She added, "You probably saved her life."

The next day, Zack was by Chloe's side when she woke. Her smile lit his world.

"Can I get you anything? Juice? Another pillow?"

She took his hand in hers. "A rain check on the wedding, I guess."

He kissed her hand. "You know I'm devoted to you even without the legal documentation that declares it. I'll put the ring on right now. I'll get the hospital chaplain to make us official."

Chloe chuckled but shook her head. "I am not getting married in a hospital after surgery. I probably look hideous."

"You're the most beautiful woman I know."

She snorted. "Love really is blind."

To prove his point, he leaned over and kissed her. The kiss was slow and sensual. When he pulled away and looked into her eyes, he saw that he'd stripped away her sadness, pain, and worry.

"Wow," she said, a little breathless, and wrapped her arms gently around him.

The memory blurred under the harsh reality of the dim

room and the bite of rope around his wrists. Would he even get the chance for a third attempt at "I do"?

~

AS THEY CONTINUED THEIR DRIVE, Chloe realized she'd spent a lot of time talking about herself. She didn't know much about Cupid, and learning about him would both enhance their relationship and distract her from the current crisis.

"What's your greatest match-making success?" she asked him.

"Oh, it's hard to pick just one. Princesses to paupers, they're all rewarding. But this isn't my story. I'm learning about you and Zack."

"Fine, but when this is over, and Zack is safe, I get to hear about the man behind the legend."

"We can do that."

Chloe bounced her left leg as she kept her right on the gas pedal. "Is Emma okay? Did she make it home from the movies?"

"One moment…. Ah, yes. Nick behaved himself."

"Good. How do you do that anyway? Can you find anyone?"

"Almost anyone, and it took hundreds of years to get good at. Not all ghosts can track people."

"Cupid's got skills."

"Tell me about when Zack proposed?"

"Hmm. How do you know I wasn't the one who proposed?"

"I know." He smiled.

Chloe thought about Zack's proposal. "He proposed on the pier. Very romantic. I remember it like it was yesterday. The night was cool but not cold, and salty air swept past us. We walked to the pier where our first date was. Golden lights were strung along the railing. As we approached, hand in hand, a quartet started playing," Chloe said wistfully.

"I'll never forget his words as his hands shook, holding the ring in it's display box. I think you know a man is committed when he's nervous in his proposal. Anyway, he said, 'Chloe, you're the most vibrant and vivacious woman I know. You are the supernova in my life, and I'd be the luckiest man to bask in the light of your life for the rest of mine.'" Goosebumps spread down her arms at the retelling.

Cupid sniffed and turned to look out the window. "Charming."

"Are you crying?"

"No."

"You teared up, didn't you?"

"Maybe." He dabbed at ghost tears under his eyes. "It was very touching. I'm a romantic, you know. It's why I do what I do—so I can be a part of the special moments in people's lives."

Chloe drove in silence as she thought of when she'd told Emma the same story. Her best friend was a massage therapist. Chloe had first met her when she'd gotten a massage at Emma's day spa. Well, not her spa. Emma hadn't owned her own place yet, but that was because Chloe hadn't yet inspired Emma to work for herself and be her own boss. She kept feeding her referrals from the gym and boosted her business.

The day Chloe told Emma about Zack's proposal, Chloe had been face down on the message table since Emma had insisted pampering herself was the best way to celebrate the happy news.

Chloe grunted from the intense pressure. "Shouldn't this be a relaxing Swedish massage to celebrate my engagement?"

"It would be—" Emma kneaded the muscles between Chloe's shoulder blade and spine "—but you're all knotted up. When was your last massage?"

"I don't know. When was the last time I came to you? Ugh, it feels like my rhomboid's being cycled through a meat grinder."

"You last came to me two years ago for a massage. Are you serious? Has it been two years?" Emma demanded.

"I've been busy," Chloe squeaked out the reply as Emma ran her forearm down her back with such force, Chloe thought her ribcage might crack.

"You need to work more self-care into your routine." She pushed directly on one of the knotted muscles.

Chloe felt the pain shoot deep before radiating outward. "Are you sure this isn't a manifestation of your frustration that I'm engaged and you're not?"

"Hmm. Tempting, but no. I really am doing deep tissue for your sake. You'll thank me later. Now, when are we going dress shopping?"

Chloe's phone chimed, bringing her back to the present. She pulled the car over to the side of the road and yanked the phone from her console.

"It's from Zack," she told Cupid with excitement. She read it aloud, "Ran into car trouble. Can you pick me up?"

"It's not from Zack," Cupid said.

Chloe rubbed her temple, considering the ghost's words. If they had Zack, they had his phone. They could have force him to unlock it, or they could have cloned his phone.

"So ... trap?" she asked.

"Trap. They need to use you as leverage against Zack."

"Oh, they'll get me, and they'll be sorry they did."

"I've no doubt." He grinned.

"How do I play this?" She wriggled her thumbs as she held the phone, ready to text back.

"I've no idea." Cupid pointed two thumbs at himself. "Ghost of love, not hostage negotiations."

"Right. K-k. But you can see the future—or parts of it?"

"Yes." He answered hesitantly as though afraid of what she was scheming. "But if you play this wrong, they might put additional, *physical* pressure on Zack to comply."

"Tell me this—is it better for me to send something like 'K-k, I'm on my way'—which I don't think they'll to believe anyway because if your rideshare breaks down, you just get another rideshare and none of that explains a two hour delay. Or, do I creep them out with a different message?"

"Let me look into this..."

Chloe waited while Cupid sat with eyes closed, channeling whatever supernatural things ghosts channeled. In the quiet, she had a moment to contemplate panicking over how she was taking advice from the ghost of love while driving toward a kidnapping and considering a rescue. She swallowed back her worry. Focus now, panic later.

At last, he told her, "Make it creepy. The creepier, the better."

"Excellent." With a maniacal grin, Chloe typed her reply and hit send.

Then she turned to Cupid. "I'm going to need a few more pieces of information from you."

Six

Zack was flexing his legs to keep them limber when Brute burst into the room, eyes flashing beneath the ski mask he wore.

"What the hell does this mean?"

Zack's eyes adjusted to the light on the screen of the phone as he read the text message.

One, two, Chloe's gonna get you.

"Does she know we have you or is she messing with you?" Brute demanded.

"I don't see how she could know you've abducted me. But she wouldn't direct something like that at me. She hates horror movies. She had nightmares from just the *Freddy Krueger* movie trailers as a child."

Loafers entered the room. "Your phone is inactive. No one can trace us here." His phone beeped with an incoming text, and he pulled the phone from his pocket.

As Loafers read the message aloud, Zack thought his face went ashen based on the parts of his face he could see through the eye holes in the mask. He held the phone for the other man to see.

"*Three, four, you're gonna hit the floor*. How'd she get your number?"

Another beep—this time Brute's phone, different from the cloned phone he initially held. "*Five, six, bury you in the sticks.*" Brute's knuckles whitened around the phone as he read, like he expected the screen itself to bite him.

Cursing, the men dashed out of the room, slamming the door behind them.

Zack sat under the dim light, wondering how this was possible. Part of him hoped Chloe was orchestrating the percolating of fear through the kidnappers, and that she was arranging some type of rescue. Part of him wanted her stowed away somewhere safe.

CHLOE BURST out laughing as Cupid told her the reaction of Zack's captors. The laugher felt good, though her insides were still churning with intense worry for Zack.

"I thought they might wet their britches," he added.

"I would've liked to have seen their faces."

"Well played, Chloe. Well played. You've managed to thoroughly confuse and worry them. You still need to rescue Zack tonight. Look at me," he shook his head, "I'm helping a woman maneuver a kidnapping. You're a first for me. And that's saying something when you've been around as long as I have."

"You might change your MO after this and join SWAT."

"Certainly not. This is far more adventure and suspense than I want for the next century."

"You've got the skills to be anything you want to be."

"'With great power comes great responsibility.'"

"Huh. I wouldn't have pegged you for a Spiderman fan."

He blinked at her. "That quote is from Voltaire, 1793."

Chloe chuckled at herself. "Well, I never claimed to have any literary knowledge."

Cupid turned to face the road, trying to feign annoyance, but she saw the upturned corners of his mouth in amusement.

"Onward?" Chloe put the car back in gear.

"'*Once more unto the breach*!'" Cupid declared.

"Ah, Shakespeare. I know that one."

"Yes, we Brits do love our Shakespeare."

They headed north on I-680, into the night, toward Zack.

CUPID LEFT CHLOE while she drove, and he arrived back at the isolated home where Zack was being held. The cybersecurity expert appeared to be making snail-pace progress on his ropes.

Unseen, the ghost walked through the door into the kitchen. He followed the sound of voices of dissension to the front living room and passed over cables running from one wall to a table near a worn, brown sofa. The table held two large computer monitors attached to a CPU and a keyboard. Beside the keyboard were a pile of ski masks and two handguns—9mm if he had to guess.

And Cupid would have to guess because he knew nothing about guns.

He looked back down at the floor. Ethernet wires. The kidnappers must have taken time and planning to set up this location.

Four men were in the confined space. One lounged on the couch, watching a soccer match on mute. Of the three men standing and bickering, one was dressed smartly in a navy suit and loafers. The other two were in black fatigues.

Cupid picked up names as he eavesdropped. The well dressed German was Erik, the large bulky man was Dolph, and the one dipping snuff was Pork.

"We don't have the woman, so we need a new plan," Dolph said.

"The backup plan is we torture the cybersecurity captive. It'll need to be something without much blood loss, and he'll need to still be able to see the screen and type," Erik explained.

Cupid's stomach rolled. This was most definitely not his domain. He was puppy dogs and heart shaped confetti. Not weapons and blood.

"Don't you have tools?" Pork asked Dolph

"I brought what I needed to rough up his fiancé who doesn't need consciousness, eyesight, and fingers."

A wave of nausea pummeled through Cupid at the image of something horrible happening to Chloe. But he didn't want Zack to suffer either.

"We"l look around the house. See what we can use," Erik said.

Cupid decided to do the same. What could he do to derail their plans—or at least delay them? He scanned the living room, eyes falling on the computer and robust trail of wires.

Perfect.

Like most ghosts, Cupid could disrupt electrical systems—trip fuses, dim lights, turn televisions to static, drop internet connections, and even shut off power. He plunged both hands into the CPU. With his full concentration and ghostly force, he shut down the system.

The TV flickered, the lights dimmed for a second, and every man in the room glanced up at the ceiling like it might fall. The effort made him dizzy.

"What the—?" Pork rushed to the table and punched buttons on the keyboard in irritation.

"What happened?" Erik demanded.

"The system shut down. I'll have to restart it."

"If we don't have a computer and internet, our plan implodes," Dolph said.

"I know. I know. I'm working on it. I don't understand what happened."

The disruption was temporary, but Cupid had bought Zack a little time. His ghostly powers may have to come back periodically to continue to disrupt the computer and delay their insidious plans for Zack.

Cupid returned to Chloe as she drove.

"Everything okay?" she asked.

"Zack is still unharmed. We need to discuss our rescue plan."

"I'm ready."

. . .

ON THE DRIVE toward Rio Vista Junction where Zack was being held, Chloe and Cupid had talked through three dozen rescue scenarios. They finally found one which didn't end in flaming disaster for Chloe and Zack. But it did involve fireworks.

"Why is Zack being held at an old house in the middle of nowhere?" Chloe asked.

"I suppose because it's remote but still has internet access. Again, ghost of love, not rescue missions."

"What can you tell me about the kidnappers?"

"They all have criminal records. The leader knew someone who'd pulled off a cyber-heist, so he thought he'd try one. They've been stalking your husband for months, scheming the kidnapping. They set up the house well in advance. My understanding is that they'd planned on taking you and Zack simultaneously from separate locations. Then neither of you could alert the other. But an accident on the bridge caused traffic to back up which prevented the second team from getting to you before you left."

She smirked. "And because you warned me. That shook up their plans."

"Yes. Once it became obvious they weren't going to find you to leverage your well-being and make Zack comply with hacking True Health's database, they went into discussions on another plan." His voice turned dismal.

Chloe swallowed. "Hurting Zack."

Cupid scrubbed hands across his face. "I don't understand this kidnapping nonsense. Why wouldn't they just hire someone to hack a backdoor to the data if they have the money for this elaborate scheme?"

Chloe blew out a slow breath. "It's complicated. And

there's no 'hacking a backdoor.' A backdoor is a programmed security flaw—the programmer can *access* a backdoor, but people don't hack into it. Zack wouldn't have built that into True Health's system anyway. The kidnappers would have to have a hacker to attempt a security breach. And hacking is a lot more complex than it seems in the movies. Zack has explained it to me before."

At Cupid's raised eyebrows, she continued, "First, a hacker would have to break through the initial firewall. This only gets him or her as far as the DMZ."

"DMZ?"

"Demilitarized zone. The DMZ consists of health system applications but not sensitive data like patient information. Then, there is another firewall between the DMZ and the patient database. And this firewall would be a different manufacturer from the first—few people would be able to hack both. If they managed to get that far, it's not as though they can just 'copy-paste' the information they want from the server."

Cupid nodded in understanding. "They picked Zack because he set up True Health's security."

"Right. He knows the layers required to get all the way to the data. He doesn't have to 'hack' anything or use a 'backdoor'. He can use administrative access and walk right through the front door. He may even be able to suspend the firewall, get to the server, and copy-paste the data."

Cupid's face fell. "They argued about how to interrogate him in a way that still kept him lucid and functional enough to navigate the internet."

"Are we going to get there before they hurt him?"

"Yes. I caused delays."

"You? What delays did you cause?"

"You've seen me flicker in and out of your car for the last half hour?"

"Yes, I thought maybe that was a ghost thing."

"I've been intermittently disrupting their power and internet access. Because of technical difficulties, they haven't had a reason to start their interrogation."

"You're not a ghost. You're a freakin' angel! No wonder people sometimes draw you with wings."

Cupid smiled. "I prefer 'reluctant hero,' but I'll take angel."

Chloe parked her car and got out for the second stop of the night and the last one before she would reach Zack. She'd first stopped at a convenience store and bought a pocket knife, lighter, and USB cable.

Now, she went inside a shady looking thrift store where Cupid had divined the store owner would be willing to sell firecrackers outside the June 28th through July 6th law in California.

"Hi." She approached the clerk counter. "I'm interested in buying Black Cat Flashlights. The one-hundred pack."

The owner, a gangly man with leathery skin and thinning hair, turned down the volume on the reality show he watched on an iPad. "By law, they don't go on sale until June 28th."

"I'm not a cop. I'm a cash paying customer."

The man ran a tongue along his teeth as he looked her up and down. He quoted her a price.

"That's double what they're worth," Cupid told her.

"That's fine." Chloe produced the cash from her purse but didn't hand it over to the man.

"How much more you got in there?" The man gave her a feral grin. He glanced leisurely around the room as if to convey she was alone with him.

Chloe clenched her teeth. "Not enough for you to get a broken nose trying to take it from me."

His eyebrows shot up but more in amusement than fear. "Is that so?"

She slammed her palm down on his countertop, startling him.

"I'm on a rescue mission! If you don't get your act together and get my firecrackers, I will beat you to a pulp and take them anyway!" She felt her cheeks flush with fury. She didn't have time to waste and meant every word—well, maybe 'to a pulp' had been an exaggeration. One of the rules of self-defense was not appearing meek or helpless. Not acting like a victim made you less likely to become one.

The man backed away from her. "Okay. Okay. They're in the back."

As he left, she turned toward Cupid. "Is he on the level or is he going to come back with a sawed-off shotgun?"

"He's getting your Black Cats only. You've made your point."

She blew out a breath as she tried to steady her nerves.

When the owner returned, they made the exchange— cash for fireworks. And he threw in some poppers for free.

Two minutes later, Chloe was out the door, in her car, and back on the road.

～

Chloe parked her car a half-mile out from the house where Zack was held captive. At least, according to Cupid, this was the location and the stealth required to approach it. She was putting a lot of faith in a ghost she'd only just met. But she did trust him.

"I'll lead you through the brush to the house," Cupid said.

Chloe didn't move.

"Chloe?"

"We're really doing this? I'm launching a rescue mission?"

His brow furrowed with worry. "We've been over the options. Calling the police will cause delays and potentially a hostage situation."

She nodded but still didn't move.

"What's wrong?" he asked.

"I don't know if I can do this. And if I don't do this, something bad could happen to Zack. If I do this and screw it up, Zack could get hurt—or worse."

"You can do this. You're a black belt."

"Sure. In sparring. I don't actually fight anyone. I teach."

"But you're trained nonetheless."

"Have you ever heard the saying *those who can't do, teach?* Well, that's me. I live in my sheltered, middle-class world where I never actually have to get physical with anyone."

Cupid turned in his seat and placed his hand on hers— through hers. "Today, that changes. Today, you'll storm that house and free your beau. Today, you'll teach those criminals they messed with the wrong fiancée."

For a moment, she imagined him having had a hundred morale boosting moments like this through the centuries, although she suspected they involved summoning the courage to court or propose, not storm a house on a rescue mission.

She took a deep breath. "K-k. Let's do this." She hopped out of the car and slammed the door shut. "I'm ready!"

Cupid lowered his chin to his chest. "Your phone, Chloe. You need your phone to call the police at the right time. And you need the Black Cats to cause a distraction."

"Right." She opened the driver's side door and grabbed her phone and firecrackers.

"We went over the plan," he said flatly.

"I know."

"Thrice."

She stretched her arms and legs. "I'm nervous."

Her mind swam with images of men wearing black with dark ski masks and guns—just as Cupid had described them.

CREEPING THROUGH THE TALL GRASS, Chloe approached the dilapidated single story farm house. The building was as Cupid described—steepled roof, white siding that was peeled and chipped, and weather-beaten shutters. Cooling AC units were jammed into various windows and padded with tacky insulation. They rattled noisily, as if working overtime to cool the house. Electrical wires criss-crossed before diving under the roof. A green

Jeep was parked beneath a slanted carport which looked like a strong wind might topple it.

Feeling a little like Macaulay Culkin from *Home Alone*, Chloe laid her traps. Poppers at the front door as well as a trip wire. The wire was actually a ten foot micro USB cable, but was the closest thing to a trip wire she found at the convenience store where she'd stopped. The poppers and wire wouldn't do more than trip and scare the kidnappers, but it was a much needed distraction as part of their choreographed plan.

According to Cupid, there were four men, two of them armed. When she came in with firecrackers blazing, two men would bolt for the front door, one would go to the back door, and the other would check the status of the hostage.

Chloe dialed 9-1-1 on her phone. When prompted to press a number if she couldn't safely speak, she did so. Then, she placed the call on mute.

She crouched outside the backdoor to the house, holding the firecrackers. "You're sure that door will bust when I kick it in?"

"Yes. The frame is rotted, so it will break the wood around the lock but not the lock itself."

"And the keys are on the kitchen counter to the left?"

"Yes. Trust me."

"K-k. Here goes nothing—or everything."

""All for love, then. Off you go." Cupid said with an encouraging smile.

Chloe unmuted her phone, slipped it in the leg pocket on the side of her yoga pants, and lit the roll of Black Cat firecrackers.

Five seconds until detonation.

She kicked in the back door, stepped inside, and hurtled the firecracker stack down the hall toward the living room where two of the men dozed in front of the TV.

Spinning back toward the kitchen, she grabbed the vehicle key just as the firecrackers erupted in what sounded like automatic gunfire.

Two men rushed out of the master bedroom. One streaked past her as she crouched in the shadows. The other spotted her and lunged for her.

Chloe dodged his big arms and jabbed an upper cut into his abdomen. He unleashed a surprised grunt.

Stumbling back, he seemed to rethink his rushed attack. This time, he readied his stance and took a more calculated swing. She rolled into him, curving around the attempted strike, and cracked her elbow into his nose. When he tried to snatch her with his hand, she ducked and glided a safe distance away.

He was bigger. She was faster.

The attacker clutched at his bleeding nose but never took his angry eyes off Chloe.

"Wait for it," Cupid told her. The man lunged for her again.

"Now!"

Chloe reached up, pulled open the freezer door, and let the man collide face first into steel. He crumpled to the floor, unconscious.

One down.

Seven

After hours of slow, painful effort, Zack had managed to liberate one wrist from the rope. He used his free hand to untie his ankles, all the while listening for sounds in case his kidnappers returned to the room they were keeping him in. The only noise was the rattling hum of the AC unit and the muffled sounds of a television. If he extricated himself from the chair, he could probably kick out the rusting AC unit and crawl out the window.

Why hadn't they yet tortured him for information? Not that he was complaining. At first, they seemed to be waiting to catch Chloe. When that failed, Zack had overheard bickering among some of the men.

An explosion of noise came from another room. Was that gunfire? Screams followed. Had the police arrived? If so, it sounded like a botched rescue. Or had the men turned on each other? That might not go well for Zack, either.

He struggled to free his last hand but wasn't fast enough before one of the kidnappers burst into the room.

Loafers.

His mask was gone and he held a gun in one hand. Even without the mask, Zack didn't recognize the man as anyone he'd seen prior to tonight, but that didn't mean they hadn't crossed paths in Zack's many travels. Somehow, Loafer's had known Zack's cybersecurity consulting job for True Health.

Loafers' eyes went wide when he saw Zack's free hand. He rushed toward Zack, and Zack remembered his self-defense training from Chloe. He kicked up his free leg, hitting the man in the groin. With an agonized groan, his aggressor fell to his knees.

Another person entered—a petite woman in a pink yoga outfit. For a wild second, Zack thought he was hallucinating.

"Chloe?" He did a double-take.

She looked down at the man writhing on the floor, clutching his injured part. "Well done," she congratulated Zack with a proud smile.

"How did you find me?"

"Explanations later. There are more bad guys out there." She pulled out a small pocket-knife and sawed through his last restraint.

His legs felt rubbery after sitting so long, but he forced them to move as he followed her to the back door. He gawked at the large man, Brute, immobile on the floor. Had Chloe done that? Was she alone?

She took his hand and led him to a Jeep parked outside.

"Their Jeep?" Where was Chloe's ride?

"My Prius is a half-mile away," she whispered. "You'd

never make it that far on foot right now, and I couldn't park any closer and give my approach away. We're taking theirs."

"Go, go," she ushered him into the passenger side. "There's one more armed kidnapper."

As he climbed in and strapped on his seatbelt, she did the same. She produced keys, started the car, and threw it into drive.

When a man stepped in front of the vehicle and took aim at them with a handgun, Chloe never slowed. Zack tensed as the gunman faced a choice—fire one round into the Jeep that might hit the driver but not in time to alter the path of the vehicle or save his own life and dodge the Jeep.

The man dove to one side. He still fired a shot, but it went wild.

Chloe let out a yip of terror, but kept the vehicle steady. Zack felt his heart threaten to pound through his chest.

"Are you okay?" she asked him.

"I'm okay." He looked down at his bleeding wrists. "I don't understand what happened back there, but I'm okay."

"I won't allow kidnappers to ruin our wedding. That's what happened."

Chloe gripped the wheel with one hand and pulled her phone from the thigh pocket of her exercise pants with the other. She spoke into it. "I'm turning my phone off now. Zack and I will drive to the station." She ended the call and put her phone back in her pocket.

"Who was that?"

"Police dispatcher." She pulled over to the side of the road where her Prius was parked.

When she climbed out of the Jeep, he followed her lead on unsteady legs. She raced around to him and threw her arms around him. Her embrace felt like a homecoming, especially since he thought he'd never see her again. Or worse, he'd see her in the hands of his kidnappers.

"Chloe." He squeezed her tight, relishing the feel of her close to him. "You could have been hurt. They had guns. What were you thinking, running a one woman rescue?"

She looked up at him, tears streaming from her eyes. "You. I was thinking about you. About what they'd do to you to get information. I couldn't trust anyone else to return you to me safely."

He smoothed her hair back from her face and kissed her forehead.

Later.

Later they could discuss this—and how she'd found him. For this moment, he wanted to cherish her. He pulled her back into a tight embrace.

"Did I ever tell you that you're the most amazing woman I know?"

WHEN CHLOE and Zack arrived at the police station, Chloe explained the situation. Sort of. Chloe told authorities she'd tracked Zack through his phone when he didn't come home. When questioned about why she didn't notify police, she explained that he was only late getting home and it was too soon to file a missing person's report. As soon as she reached where he was, she called the police. But since she couldn't see inside and suspected Zack was in imminent danger, she couldn't wait for their arrival. So she detonated some robust fireworks she found outside the house—definitely not purchased illegally by her--and went inside to rescue him.

She didn't like lying, and the police didn't seem completely satisfied by her explanation, but her *exhaustive* personality seemed to wear them down. The police informed the couple that the kidnappers were in custody when they released Chloe and Zack with a cautionary, 'we'll be back in touch.'

Explaining events to Zack on the way home was a different matter. She couldn't lie to Zack.

They didn't arrive back at home until daybreak.

Chloe tossed her keys on the counter, and Zack bolted the door.

She turned to him as she kicked off her sneakers. "Do you want the sane version I told the police or the bizarre, mind-bending truth which involves potions and a ghost named Cupid?"

He grinned. "I can't fathom how you found me. The police said you said you traced my phone, but these creeps were no amateurs. They wouldn't have left my phone on except briefly when they texted you. And how did you text their phones?"

She gave him a sheepish grin. "You're a logical man. My explanations will not be based in logic."

"I'm exhausted, and everything seems surreal. I think if you told me you rode a unicorn with a leprechaun on your shoulder to come to my rescue, I'd just accept it." He reached over and held her hand. "Let's get home, get some sleep, and tell me all about potions and Cupid tomorrow."

As Zack led her toward the bedroom, Chloe glanced over her shoulder.

Cupid leaned against the doorway, arms folded, watching them with a small, satisfied smile.

Six days left, she thought. Plenty of time to make sure they actually got to "I do."

Eight

Chloe stood in her dressing room, white gown flowing around her. Her hair was pinned up away from her face, and she wore teardrop diamond earrings.

Emma dabbed tears away from her eyes with a tissue. "I can't believe this is finally happening. And all because Aunt Rose loaned you a ghost for a week."

"I'm glad you believed my story. I lived through it, and I'm still not sure I believe what happened." A week ago she'd been pacing her kitchen, staring at a potion bottle like a lunatic. Now she stood in a gown, a ghost at her shoulder, and her entire world intact.

"Once you've seen half the bizarre things Aunt Rose does, ghosts don't seem so farfetched. And Cupid of all ghosts! Maybe he can play match-maker for me next."

Cupid appeared beside Chloe, an admiring look on his face. "I've come to wish the bride well on her special day. And what a beautiful bride you are."

"Emma, Cupid is here. Can you give us a minute so I can say goodbye?"

Emma blinked at the empty air beside Chloe—empty to her, anyway—and smiled. "Tell him I said hi." She gathered up the hem of her pink maid of honor dress and slipped out the dressing room door.

Chloe turned to Cupid and smiled. "I wish I could hug you right now. This is as far as we've ever gotten. And it's all because of you."

"You don't give yourself enough credit. You're the one who had the tenacity to make your wedding day a reality."

"Will you be there today?" Chloe asked.

"I wouldn't miss it for all the arrows in Robin Hood's quiver."

"And then you're gone?"

"And then I'm gone. Hopefully, the next time a young woman or a young man calls on me for help, it won't be such a dire situation. One nail biting, kidnapping, edge of your seat suspense is quite enough for me for the next hundred years."

Chloe nudged his apparition with her elbow. "I don't know. You might get bored."

"Love is many things, but never boring."

"Thanks again."

"Go get your beau."

A few minutes later, Chloe stood at the back of the church, arm-in-arm with her father. Soft light from stained-glass windows warmed her shoulders as she walked.

He patted her forearm. "Today's the big day."

"For real this time." Chloe couldn't stop smiling.

As the music played, her father escorted her down the

aisle. She was surrounded by both her and Zack's family and friends. Rose was in the crowd with Cupid sitting beside her. Rose winked at her, and Chloe wondered if Cupid had told her much of what had happened. Emma stood near the altar with the bridesmaids.

Then, Chloe's gaze fell on Zack, and at long last, they said their vows.

ZACK DANCED WITH HIS MESMERIZING, beautiful wife with her silken brunette hair and white dress. She looked like a princess. She was always beautiful in her exercise clothes, but today, she looked exquisite. Her entire body glowed from head to toe—his supernova.

Chloe had given an outlandish tale of how she'd rescued him the other night. She'd chatted on about a ghost and setting traps, but it all seemed impossible. And yet, he had no other explanation.

She'd even gone so far as to prove she was omniscient through Cupid by having Zack hide things in the house from her and having her 'ghost' tell her where the items were. So odd. But he'd always liked her quirks and her spunk. What mattered more than mythical creatures, was the end result. He was free, they were safe, and they had said their vows.

Chloe had been in charge of choosing the music. For their first song, she picked Sam Cooke's *Cupid*. Zack didn't need anyone to strike him or Chloe with an arrow of love like the lyrics suggested—that had already happened years ago, but the song was soothing and perfect anyway.

Of course, as long as he was dancing with his wife,

Chloe could've picked any song, and it would still have been one of the happiest days of Zack's life.

As the music wrapped around them, Zack tightened his hold on his wife. Cupid could retire for all he cared—his work here was done.

Chloe was his forever.

<<<<>>>>

***** QUICK NOTE FROM THE AUTHOR *****

READY FOR ANOTHER sweet and magical romantic suspense? There are so many delights to enjoy! Keep scrolling for the first chapter in the next book.

Romancing the Spirit

IN BOXED SETS

INDIVIDUAL BOOKS
  Romancing the Spirit Series #1
  Sadie's Spirit / Willow's Windfall
  Cassie's Chase / Phoebe's Pharaoh
  Vanessa's Valentine / Autumn's Angel
  Romancing the Spirit Series #2
  Carol's Christmas / Allison's Alibi

THE CHRISTMAS COLLECTION

Dear Reader

If you enjoyed this book and want to know about future releases by CB Samet you can CLICK HERE (or visit www.cbsamet.com) to sign up for my mailing list! I promise I won't spam you. I only send an email when I have a new book released, giveaways, or special discounts. And I'll never sell your information. You can also unsubscribe at any time.

If you enjoyed this story, kindly let others know by posing a brief comment on social media or leave a review where you purchased it.

Keep reading for excerpts from the next novella!

Thank you for reading,
   CB Samet

Other Books by CB Samet

Looking for more romantic suspense with more action and sizzle? How about with an urban fantasy twist? Check out my supernatural adventures...

The Shadow Guardians Trilogy

Urban fantasy Norse Mythology Adventure

Get *Raven's Flight, a prequel novella* for FREE. In my newsletter, you'll learn about me, special discounts, and new releases.

Raven's Flight, prequel novella

Raine Down, Book 1

Rosalyn's Run, novella

Storm Surge, Book 2

Anka's Orb, novella

Sky Fall, Book 3

Olympian Awakenings Trilogy

Urban fantasy Greek Mythology Adventure

Grab the prequel exclusively HERE.

Stone Hearts

Winds of Destiny

Flame and Shadow

Box Set 3

The Rider Files

Romantic Suspense Thrillers

Meridian File / Masters File / Box Set 1

McMillan File / Maltisse File /Box Set 2

Storm File / Sullivan File /

Sharp File / Sizani File / Box Set 4

Rivera File / Rucker File / Box Set 5

Richmond File / Redwood File / Box Set 6

Atlas File / Angel File / Box Set 7

Buy 4book box sets direct from author and save 10%

Payhip. Use code E152M0GZG4

The Dr. Whyte Adventure Novels

Thriller Series

Black Gold

Whyte Knight

Gray Horizon

Love action/adventure and strong female leads in a fantasy world? Check out my other genre:

The Avant Champion Fantasy Series

The Avant Champion: Rising

Malakai: An Avant Champion Origin of Malos Story (prequel)

SABRINA'S STORM

A woman seeking solace.
A ghost hunter seeking the truth.
And the storm that threatens both their lives.

Chapter 1 (excerpt)

Grant Dalton stared at the three-story beach house with faded wood paneling framed in gray autumn clouds rolling across a high sun. Porch steps led up to a weathered, baby-blue door. Behind the house, sand dunes stretched to the ocean with beach grass swaying in the salty breeze.

The secluded bed and breakfast made a pleasant vacation spot. Too bad Grant wasn't visiting for vacation. He had a job to do, but he would wait to move his equipment discretely inside after he toured the house and met the owner.

With his suitcase by his side, he knocked on the door. No answer. He checked his watch, noting he'd arrived forty-five minutes early. He fished in his pocket, withdrew his phone, and checked his email. The rental instructions included the key code in case he came early or if the owner was out of the vicinity.

He punched in the code, which unlocked a key holder. With the key, he let himself inside the house.

"Hello?"

No answer came, but the chandelier in the dining room to his left shuddered as if opening the door had created a stiff breeze.

Curious, he thought.

No lights were on, but sunlight shone through the windows on either side. Yet the house still felt shadowy—dim, and a bit lonely. The dark, stained floors and wood wall paneling made the foyer seem small, but the aged wood looked restored.

He'd spent time in creepy, dilapidated houses. This one was cared for, though he'd expected as much based on the online photos. Still, the decor lacked warmth or personal touches—pictures, paintings, or even a bouquet of flowers. So, it neither felt warm and cozy like a beach rental house, nor appeared decrepit and worn like a haunted house.

Grant carried his luggage up the stairs, first door on the left, to his rented room. Now *this* was a bed and breakfast room. Oak framed paintings of beaches and ships at sea hung on sky-blue walls.

One acrylic in particular caught his eye—a ship with an albatross flying above it. He wondered if it had been inspired by *The Rime of the Ancient Mariner*. He knew the poem well from a paper he'd written ten years ago in college English.

The ship was cheered, the harbour cleared,
Merrily did we drop
Below the kirk, below the hill,
Below the lighthouse top.

The bedspread was forest green with compasses and nautical ropes. A dozen plump, decorative pillows lay at the head of the bed.

Interesting. Maybe the owner had some type of pillow fetish.

A desk and chair against one wall held a small envelope. He opened it and read the note.

Thank you for staying at Oceanside Bed and Breakfast. Breakfast is served daily at eight am and dinner at six pm. Please give me a day's advance notice if you need different meal times. Clean towels are in the bathroom. The desk can be moved onto the balcony during the day for writing inspiration.
Sincerely, your host,
Sabrina Morningstar

He admired the penmanship and personal touch. She'd remembered he had listed the purpose of his 'vacation' as writing time. He hadn't lied—he did need time to write. He hoped to put pen to paper (or fingers to keyboard) while he was here, but personal writing wasn't his primary objective.

Sabrina wouldn't know his true purpose until the

opportune time—on camera. On that note, he needed to get his video equipment out of his vehicle discretely while no one else was there. But maybe he could take a moment to enjoy the balcony view. One of the joys of his job was traveling, so he was sure to enjoy the scenery. Few places he'd visited had such a splendid view as this.

He stepped outside to a pleasant October ocean breeze. Beneath a now completely overcast sky, the water was a choppy sapphire. The beach sloped up toward the house, and a sun-bleached gray walkway bridged the erosion dune to connect house and beach. In the backyard, a raised garden grew squash, cauliflower, lettuce, and Brussel sprouts.

With the wind in his hair and salt on his tongue, Grant realized this was probably the nicest 'haunted' house he'd ever stayed in. Too bad he'd never stay again. Once he revealed peoples' fraudulent claims of their tourist-trap houses harboring ghosts, people tended to want to never see him again. Some even went as far as restraining orders and threats. He wasn't sure why—he wasn't the criminal in these scenarios.

The beach had been deserted until Grant noticed a jogger. A woman with platinum blonde hair kept close to the surf, running in the compact sand but still leaving a trail of prints. She appeared to be close to his age, about thirty. She stopped at the beach parallel to the house and began to strip.

He took a step back and glanced nervously around. He wasn't voyeuristic, and this woman obviously thought she was relaxing alone. When he glanced back in her direction, his tension eased as he noticed her white swimsuit against tan skin. She had an hour-glass figure, drawing his eyes to a narrow waist and muscular thighs.

She pulled a kayak from the beach into the surf. After wading hip deep into the water, she climbed in the boat and began paddling. He shuddered for her—the water was probably sixty-five degrees, but maybe the coolness felt refreshing after a long run.

Had it been a long run? He looked up and down the beach, wondering where she'd come from and if she lived nearby or visited on vacation.

Didn't matter. He wasn't here to meet a woman. Not exactly. He was here to expose a fraud—Sabrina Morningstar.

Sabrina toweled off and sat on the beach after her paddling. The waves had given her a robust workout. Resting back on her elbows, she watched the slate clouds moving briskly overhead. The vast Atlantic Ocean churned before her. She loved the expanse of it—water as far as the eye could see with no buildings obstructing the view.

She could look into the ocean for hours and feel small and insignificant. Doing so made her problems feel small and insignificant as well. When she mentally shrank them to a manageable size in this way, they fit nicely into something the size of a small jewelry box she could lock away until they outgrew their prison once again.

When her phone rang, she fished it out of her shorts pocket in the pile of clothes beside her. "Hi, Lee Ann."

"Sabrina, how are you?" her sister asked.

"I'm good. What's up?"

Sabrina recognized her sister's familiar patterns. If she launched into her day at work, then Sabrina knew she wanted casual conversation. If Lee Ann opened with a question, then she was all business.

"It's mid-October. We haven't heard if you're coming to Thanksgiving this year."

"I'm not sure. I might get a late renter." Truthfully, Sabrina wasn't sure she possessed the emotional fortitude for a large family gathering. Half of them would know what happened—or some version of a passed around story. They'd give her wide berth with looks of pity. The other half wouldn't know her story and so would ask her how a job she didn't have any more was treating her.

Not good. Not good at all.

"Well, Mom's up my butt to find out if you're coming. What do you want me to tell her?"

Her mom would set her younger sister to pester her.

"Tell her I don't yet know." Sabrina could know. She could simply mark the dates on the online rental calendar as 'unavailable.' But since she kept dumping money into the beach house repairs, she needed rentals.

Maybe the writer coming today would find inspiration and stay longer. After all, he'd insisted on renting all three bedrooms so he could have the peace and quiet he desired. Odd, since peace and quiet waited a short walk away at the beach, but because he was paying, she wasn't going to tell him what to do. Also, one person meant smaller meals to fix, and therefore a smaller grocery bill for the 'all-inclusive' meal part of her bed and breakfast.

"Sabrina?"

"Yeah?"

"You have to let it go." Lee Ann's voice was part pleading, part demanding.

If only letting go of the past was so simple. "I'm trying."

"Just decide to let it go, and then it will be gone."

"Like flipping a switch?" Sabrina's question came out harsher than she'd intended.

"It's been over a year," her sister pressed.

Three hundred seventy-two days to be exact. Three hundred seventy-two days Sabrina had stolen from Patrick's life.

"I'm trying," she repeated.

She said goodbye, disconnected the call, and headed back toward the house, carrying her kayak and paddle.

Grant enjoyed the sea breeze until a sudden grating noise behind him had him spinning around. The glass balcony door slid shut.

"What the—?" He tried to pull it back open, but the latch wouldn't budge. He looked through the glass into the room but saw no one.

His heart pounded until he took a few deep breaths to steady himself. He'd been trapped inside spooky rooms more times than he could count. No cause for alarm. He tugged on the door again. This was a convincing trick—no doubt engineered to maintain the illusion of a haunted house.

He banged on the door a few times, feeling his irritation mount. But unleashing his frustration on the glass door wasn't going to budge the lock, so he reigned in his temper.

Moving away from the sliding door, he looked over the balcony. He could climb the rail and lower himself down to the first-floor balcony, but he wasn't certain the rail would hold his weight as he clung to it. He was stuck waiting for the hostess to return home.

"Please don't jump. You'll only hurt yourself," a female voice said.

He whirled around to the open balcony door where a woman stood—the same woman from the beach. She had a round face with dark blue eyes, like stormy waters, rimmed in dark mascara. She wore a silver necklace and the same running clothes he'd seen her in on the beach.

"Mr. Dalton?" she asked.

He cleared his throat. "Yes. And you are?"

"Sabrina Morningstar." She extended a hand.

He blinked as he shook it. This was Sabrina? He'd imagined an old, withered widow running this beach-based bed and breakfast.

"I see you found your room." Her smile was positively disarming.

"Yes." He took his hand back and straightened.

Good looks aside, he was here on the job. He was here to debunk the claims that this was a haunted house, and this little stunt she'd just pulled with the door only strengthened his resolve.

He eyed her before inspecting the door, sliding it back and forth. "The door shut on me."

Her mouth formed a surprised oh, and he instantly

disliked the way the fullness of her lips drew his gaze toward them.

"I'm sorry." She began inspecting the base. "I checked with a level to see if there's a slant to the house which might have caused this, but it's even. Then, I replaced the door two months ago. I don't know why this keeps happening."

"I'm not the first?"

"No."

"What about the lock?" he asked.

When she gave him a confused look, he explained, "I was locked outside." He kept his voice firm, perhaps a bit accusatory, as he leveled his gaze at her.

She looked up at him with a quirk of her lips. "I'm afraid that's impossible, Mr. Dalton." She glanced down at the door handle. "There is no lock."

<<CONTINUE THE ADVENTURE>>